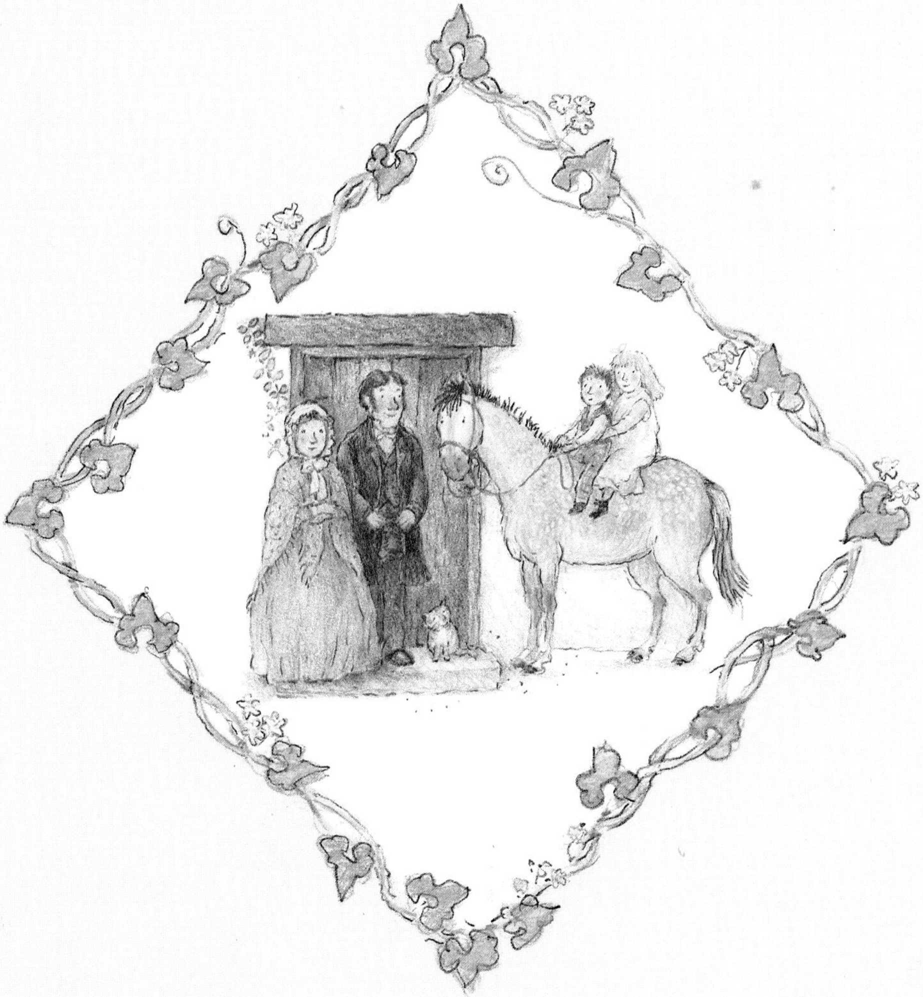

For Mary Usher
P. & E.R.

For John
P.L.

Text copyright © 1991 by Paul and Emma Rogers
Illustrations copyright © 1991 by Priscilla Lamont

First U.S. edition 1993
First published in Great Britain in 1991 by Walker Books Ltd., London.

Library of Congress Cataloging-in-Publication Data:

Rogers, Emma.
Our house / Emma and Paul Rogers :
illustrated by Priscilla Lamont.—1st U.S. ed.

Summary: A look at the different families that have lived
in a house during the two hundred years since it was first built.

[1. Dwellings—Fiction. 2. Family life—Fiction.]
I. Rogers, Paul, 1950- . II. Lamont, Priscilla, ill. III. Title.
PZ7.R6279Ou   1993 [E]—dc20   92-53015
ISBN 1-56402-134-3

10 9 8 7 6 5 4 3 2 1

Printed in Hong Kong

The pictures in this book were done in
pencil and colored pencil.

Candlewick Press
2067 Massachusetts Avenue
Cambridge, Massachusetts 02140

Our House

Emma and Paul Rogers
illustrated by Priscilla Lamont

CANDLEWICK PRESS
CAMBRIDGE, MASSACHUSETTS

1780

Welcome

This is the story of an old old house that
once was new. It begins in the springtime,
in the days before bulldozers and trucks
and cranes, before concrete blocks
or ready-made window frames.

The quiet of the valley, along the narrow
country path, rings with the stone mason's
hammer, the carpenter's saw, and the cries
of the children rolling in the straw.

Week by week, month by month,
the day draws nearer when the family
will move in. Joe, the littlest one,
is the most excited of all.

The house is ready in the autumn.
For luck, Father carries Mother over the
threshold. "Mother! Mother!" says Joe. "I
planted an acorn in the yard! Who'll grow
big first? The oak tree or me?"

Soon the house becomes
a home. Joe and his sister and
brother know every corner of it—
every nook and cranny.

But Joe has one favorite place. On winter
evenings he curls up in the chimney seat.
"My seat, my tree, our home," thinks Joe.
"Welcome," says the house.

1840

Father's Late

Sixty years have come and gone.
Joe has long since grown up. A doctor and his
family live here now. Tonight he's ridden
out on his horse to see a patient far away.
For these are the days before cars.

In the house Thomas and
Meg wait anxiously. They listen
for the clatter of his horse outside.
"Father's late," they whisper.

The thunder roars. Lightning flashes
across the sky. Out on the road, Father
struggles against the storm. "Keep going, Bess,"
says Father. "We'll soon be home."

The wind tears at the oak tree and
rattles the roof tiles. The rain lashes
the windows of the house. "Poor Father."
The children sigh. "Where can he be?"

The sun wakes Thomas and Meg
in the morning. They run around to the
back of the house, picking up windfalls.
"Look!" shouts Meg. "A branch from the
tree is down!" Suddenly they hear hooves in the
yard. "Father's back!" they call. "Quick,
bring some apples for Bess!"
"As I rode through the storm," says Father,
"I thought of you all, safe at home."
"Wherever you go," says the house,
"I'll be waiting here."

1910

Wait and See

Seventy winters, seventy
summers more. A new fence, new roof tiles,
new faces. For one little girl, Sophie,
today is a special day.

Inside the house, there's the smell of new bread. Out in the yard, freshly-washed clothes billow on the line. Everyone's busy, scrubbing and dusting and ironing.

Grandpa has a secret.

He's working in the shed.

"What are you making?" Sophie asks.

"Wait and see!" Grandpa says.

"Happy birthday, Sophie!"
the guests say as they arrive.
"Come and see my new baby brother,"
Sophie says. "He's fast asleep in his crib."

"There's something else new," Father
tells them. "Hot and cold water upstairs!"
And while Father shows off the bathroom,
Grandpa shows Sophie his secret.

A swing for Sophie's birthday!
They hang it from the old oak tree.
"I want to live here all my life," says Sophie.
The house says, "Wait and see."

1990

Where's Henry?

It's been eighty years since that day.
Now who plays in the garden? Who lives
in the house now? It's Polly. She's drawing
a picture while Henry, her pet mouse,
plays in his cage.

"Oh no! Henry escaped,"
Polly wails. "Where can he be?"
There are more hiding places in this old
house than anyone would believe.

"What's that noise in the cupboard?" asks Mom.

"Maybe he's hiding inside the piano," says Polly.

"I can hear something up here," says Dad.

"We'll have to pull up a floorboard or two."

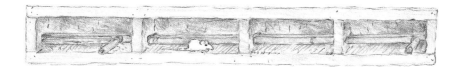

"Hey, look at this funny doll I found!" calls Dad.
"What's this?" says Mom. "It's some kind of saw.
And who do you think this pipe belonged to?
Someone who lived here before?"

"Old things!" thinks Polly. "Nobody
looked in the attic! Henry could be up there."
As she opens the trap door, she hears something
scratching in the corner. "Got him!" Polly says.

That night she draws a new picture and pushes
it down the crack behind the chimney seat.
"I wonder who will find it," she whispers.
"Time will tell," says the house.

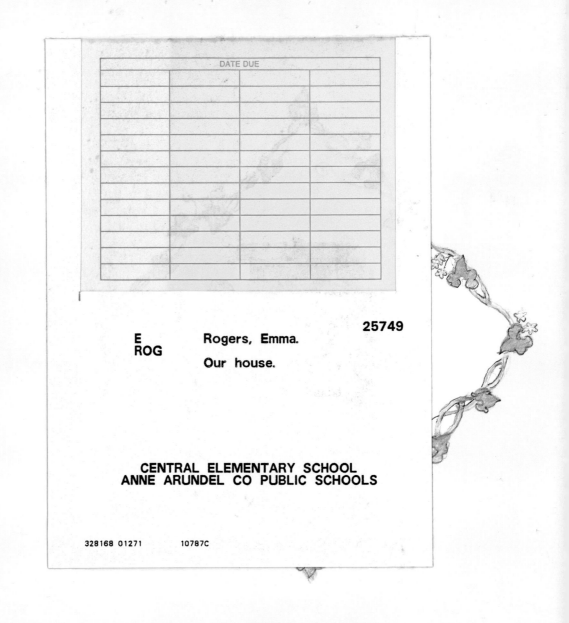

DATE DUE			

25749

E
ROG

Rogers, Emma.

Our house.

CENTRAL ELEMENTARY SCHOOL
ANNE ARUNDEL CO PUBLIC SCHOOLS